W9-APB-715

THE Golden Stallion

(Abridged)

By RUTHERFORD MONTGOMERY

Illustrated by AL BRULÉ

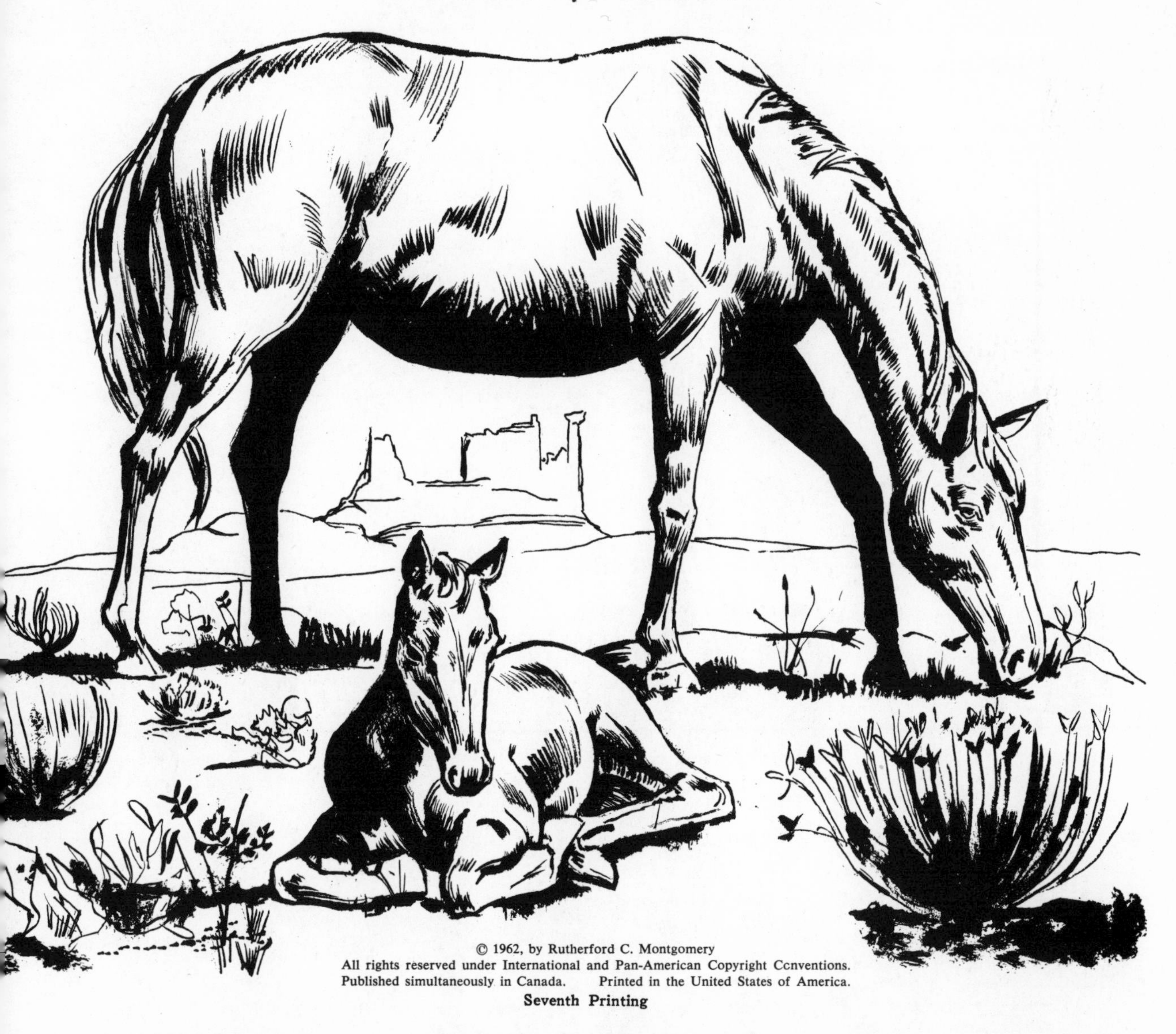

Seventh Printing

GROSSET & DUNLAP • Publishers • NEW YORK

HIGH COUNTRY

CHARLIE CARTER of the Bar L ranch was looking for a renegade silvertip, a bear with a price upon his head because in his old age he had turned to stock killing. Hibernation the fall before had saved him from the wrath of the Bar L riders. Now it was early spring, and the old bear would be on the loose again.

Charlie was riding up a narrow canyon. He was sure the bear was holed up in a den above the canyon rim. He was riding Patric, because Patric was stone deaf and did not mind having a rifle fired over his head. Charlie was only a boy, but he could ride a horse and shoot a rifle as well as any of the men.

Patric was taking it easy. He had halted and was standing with his head down. Charlie was watching a snow bank above on a rim. The slopes of Sleepy Cat Mountain were covered with deep banks of snow which would soon be melting. Charlie roused Patric and they moved on.

As they neared the mouth of the canyon Charlie's hand dropped to the butt plate of his rifle which was shoved into a leather boot under his right stirrup flap. Close above him great drifts jutted out from the steep side of the mountain. Charlie knew that his father would not have liked his entering the canyon if he had known about it, because this was slide time, when the mountain's soggy snow could break loose and plunge into the canyon, bringing with it rocks and trees. But he wanted very much to be the one who took the old bear.

Then he suddenly spotted the bear. He was following a ledge close to the rim of the canyon, plowing along through the wet snow, pausing often to scoop up some of the snow and swallow it.

Charlie decided that he would have to chance a long shot when the silvertip reached the closest point above him. His big game rifle was deadly at up to four hundred yards. That was a long shot, but he had made longer ones.

The bear moved along, not bothering to keep to cover. Charlie raised his rifle and tested the sights on the bear. When the silvertip was directly above him, he squeezed the trigger. When the blast of the rifle rang out, the bear whirled and faced down country. Charlie worked the rifle's lever to reload, knowing he had undershot his target. At that moment Patric came to life. Whirling about, the horse plunged away. He had seen a massive lip of snow break loose as the bear leaped out upon it, alerted by the rifle shot. Charlie glanced upward and saw a mass of snow, rocks and trees plunging down into the canyon. He let Patric have his head.

A great roar, like that of a fast train, filled Charlie's ears, and the ground shook under Patric's flying hoofs. The horse strained every muscle as he leaped forward. Trees and rocks and dirty snow boiled over the rim and shot downward. Charlie forgot about the bear; forgot everything except the effort Patric was making to escape the falling death. Patric plunged out of the canyon a second before the avalanche plunged into it.

Charlie had caught a brief glimpse of the bear being swallowed by

the slide, and knew that the silvertip's raiding days were over. He headed Patric toward home. No one would claim the reward for killing the bear, for there would be nothing left to make a claim. But the Bar L calves would be safe.

Riding over a ridge, Charlie saw the Bar L buildings below. There were a rambling two-story log ranch house, a big new barn, a bunk house, a saddle house and two large corrals. Below the building spread the home pastures dotted with cows and calves, and closer to the big barn was the horse pasture. It was a familiar scene, for he had been born there.

Charlie urged Patric to a gallop, and as he rode he thought of how to tell his father about his experience. As they passed the horse pasture, he whistled to his saddle mare, a trim black. From now on he would ride Trey Spot. She was a fast horse and had won the big race at last fall's valley rodeo. The boys at the Bar L had doubted Trey Spot. She was too slender-barreled, too light in the legs. But she had run away from the fastest horses entered. Charlie was very proud of her.

Charlie didn't get to tell about the bear. When he entered the house, he learned that his mother was ill. Nothing serious, but she must not be excited. Ann Carter, his mother, was an outdoor woman and would certainly have been excited about the escape from the canyon. After eating a sandwich and drinking a glass of milk, Charlie returned to the horse corral. He whistled Trey Spot in from the pasture and saddled her, then he rode away from the ranch. He had another job he wanted to do.

Charlie was glad his father had not had time to talk to him. Grandby Carter was a big man and easygoing, but he did not believe in taking foolish chances such as entering a narrow canyon when slides were due to run. Charlie's problem had to do with a band of wild horses Tex Malone, the range boss, had reported seeing on Bar L range. The herd would eat up grass needed by the Bar L cattle and horses.

None of the ranchers liked wild horses. The mares were usually scrubs with a scrub stallion bossing them. According to Tex, the way to handle an invasion of wild horses was with a rifle or a call to meat hunters who would round them up and sell them to a slaughterhouse for dog meat. However, Charlie Carter loved horses too much to allow even scrubs to be sent to a slaughterhouse.

But he was in no hurry. He liked to watch the small and big dwellers of the high country, the big fat whistlers, cousins of the woodchuck, the golden mantle chipmunks, the chickaree squirrels, the big rabbits, now changing to their summer coat of gray, the pairs of coyotes, and an occasional bobcat or cougar.

Charlie halted on a ridge and looked down upon a bench bordered by aspen trees with new leaves just turning green. At the upper end of the bench he saw two horses. He had found the herd. Now he must work carefully so as to find out how big the herd was. If disturbed they would disappear quickly, and he needed to know how many there were.

He did not ride close to the two horses, but headed for high ground. He halted in a spot from which he could see all of the bench without being seen. Now all he had to do was to keep Trey Spot from sounding off and warning the wild horses. He turned her so that she could not look down upon the bench.

Charlie counted eighteen mares, but he had not seen the stallion he knew would be boss of the herd. After a short wait, the stallion broke cover. He was a big red fellow with a shaggy spring coat, a real horse in spite of his scarred and battered appearance. He was ugly, but there was a strange, primitive beauty in his powerful body.

As he watched the stallion, he understood why this herd had escaped the meat hunters. Their leader had intelligence and courage, that was certain. Charlie noted that some of the mares carried brands, which meant that they had been stolen from ranch herds.

The mares were grazing, moving toward the spot where Charlie sat. Suddenly Trey Spot scented them and sounded off with an eager whinny. The stallion whirled and looked toward the grove where Charlie was hidden. Then he laid back his ears and screamed savagely. Charlie pulled Trey Spot around and sent her down the slope at a gallop. It was time to stampede the herd over the pass and out of Bar L territory.

The stallion lunged at the nearest mare and slashed her rump with his teeth. Instantly the herd bunched and fled toward the pass above. Trey

Spot increased her pace and began closing the gap between herself and the big red stallion who was behind the mares.

She was close upon the heels of the stallion when another horse galloped out of a stand of spruce. The newcomer was a colt, golden yellow in color. His mane and tail were blond and streamed in the wind like spun gold. The instant he appeared, the leader swerved and charged toward him.

Charlie knew the leader had driven the young stallion out of the herd, but probably the youngster wasn't quite ready to strike out for himself. The colt swerved and fled with graceful speed down toward the bench. The sight made Charlie's pulse quicken. He pulled Trey Spot around and sent her after the colt. The big red stallion turned back to his job of stampeding the mares.

Charlie knew he was going to try to rope the colt. The little stallion would be a prize worth capturing. As they pounded along, Charlie shook out his rope. Suddenly he was aware that Trey Spot was not overtaking the colt. The golden streak up ahead was actually running away from the mare, and doing it with effortless ease.

By the time they reached the timber at the lower end of the bench, the colt had gained ten lengths on Trey Spot. Charlie pulled the mare up to let her blow. As he coiled his rope he smiled. He had decided to change all of his plans for the herd. He would let them stay on Bar L range until he had captured the colt. He'd convince his father and have him tell Tex not to go after the wild horses.

As he rode toward home, he thought about the red stallion. He had heard his mother and father speak of a great red stallion they had seen several times. The range riders called him Big Red. They had once tried to rope him, but had failed.

PLANS

THAT night at supper Charlie felt good. His mother was up and looked well. She smiled at him.

"Where have you been all day?" she asked.

"I covered a bit of country," he answered.

His father frowned. "There's ranch work to be done before you go chasing around."

"I checked on the wild herd," Charlie said.

"Locate them?" Tex asked.

Charlie nodded as he helped himself to steak. "There's a golden colt with them, a honey."

Shorty Spears, the horse wrangler, was instantly interested. "A sure-enough palomino?" he asked.

"Hundred percent," Charlie said with a wide grin. "He outran Trey Spot ten lengths over three-quarters of a mile."

"Ten lengths?" Ann Carter asked eagerly.

"Reckon I better round him up and race him this fall," Shorty said.

"He's my horse. I spotted him," Charlie said.

"How many in the herd?" Carter asked.

"Eighteen mares, a tough old boss who is some horse himself, and the golden colt," Charlie answered.

"If he's as good as you say, he must be branded," his father said.

"He's never had an iron on him." Charlie was positive. "He grew up with that herd and now the red stallion is trying to run him off."

"This red stallion," Grandby questioned. "Will he give us trouble?"

"I'm afraid he will," Charlie admitted. "He's bigger than Kelly, and he's as smart as he is mean. But I like him."

"You know we're going to run the mares on the upper range with Kelly. Will a fence stop this fellow?"

Charlie looked his father in the eye. "A fence won't stop him. He has five branded mares in his herd now."

"What do you suggest?" Grandby put it squarely to his son.

"I'll make it so hot for him that he'll stay on the south side of the pass," Charlie replied.

Tex didn't say anything, but there was a gleam in his eye. He knew how to handle the brute. He'd use his saddle carbine and save a lot of time and energy.

Charlie caught the gleam in Tex's eye. "Don't do any shooting until I have a chance," he begged.

"There'll be no shooting, Tex. That's an order," Grandby said sternly.

"And while I'm at it, I'll catch the colt. He's mine. I was the first to spot him," Charlie said.

"Does the red stallion have a cropped ear and a white diamond on his forehead?" Ann Carter asked.

"Yes," Charlie admitted.

"It must be Big Red." Ann Carter was excited.

"Could be, but he'd be pretty old," Tex said. "It would explain why Hackett and his meat hunters haven't rounded up the herd."

Grandby shook his head. He doubted if the stallion was Big Red.

Charlie's mother took a letter from her sweater pocket. "Ellen Sprague is coming out to spend the summer on the ranch." She smiled at Charlie. Ellen was about Charlie's age and liked to ride. Her mother was an old friend of Ann Carter.

Charlie wasn't much interested. He was thinking about the golden colt, already planning on how he'd catch him.

ROPE HAND

CHARLIE drove into town to meet Ellen. While he was waiting for the train to arrive, he went to Boone's hardware store to purchase some supplies. Two men were talking near a counter. Charlie knew both of them. One was a wild-horse hunter named Hackett, the other was a Slash T cowhand. The Slash T cowboy said:

"When you bringing that plane in, Hackett?"

"Soon as Buck Kent gets it fixed up." Kent was a red-faced man with hunched-over shoulders.

"Tough country for a plane," the cowboy said.

"Buck can fly any place. He gets the meat every time," Hackett said as he blew out a puff of smoke from his cigar.

"Got a horse herd spotted?" the Slash T man asked.

"Yeah," Hackett answered. "I've spotted a big red stallion with a bunch of mares. Buck will cut the stallion out of the herd and I'll knock him down with my rifle. The rest will be easy."

"Shoot from the plane?" the cowboy asked.

"Easy," Hackett said. "Buck will dive in on him and I'll let him have it."

"Sounds real sporting." The lank cowboy turned away from Hackett and his high heels clicked as he walked away.

Hackett scowled as he turned to the clerk back of the counter.

"I'm doing the ranchers a good turn, getting wild horses off the range," he said.

"Where is this herd?" the clerk asked. He wanted to be polite.

"Up on the bench above the Bar L, I guess. They were heading that way," Hackett answered.

Charlie picked up the box of cartridges Mr. Booth had placed on the counter. The horse hunter was talking about Big Red and his herd. Charlie's lips tightened. He'd have to do something about the herd or they would all be killed, including the golden colt.

As they rode back to the ranch, Ellen noticed that Charlie did not have much to say. She wondered why he looked grim, but did not ask him.

Charlie was glad to have Ellen visiting. It gave him a good excuse for riding up to the horse range. He was supposed to show Ellen the ranch. She told him she had ridden a great deal in her home in the East, but he planned to be careful in picking a horse for her.

"I'll let you ride Trey Spot," Charlie said as they stood at the corral gate the day after Ellen's arrival. "I'll ride Mother's horse, Diamond."

"I want to learn everything—how to rope a calf and things like that." Ellen spoke eagerly. She made a nice picture with her corn-colored hair fluffing out under the Stetson hat. Charlie grinned at her.

"Trey Spot is an expert rope horse," he said.

As they rode toward the cow pasture, Charlie made plans. After they had spent some time letting Ellen try roping a calf, they could ride up for a quick trip to the benches where the wild horses were.

The cow pasture was the biggest pasture Ellen had ever seen. It extended for a mile north and south and was three-quarters of a mile wide. They entered a ravine, and as they rounded a clump of willows, their horses stopped abruptly. In the trail ahead of them stood a white-faced bull. He was a yearling and he had his head down as he pawed at the turf. His bellow echoed across the gully.

"What's the matter with him?" Ellen asked.

Charlie saw the quills in the bull's lips and muzzle. "He mixed with a porcupine," he said.

"Poor thing. Will he let us pull them out?" Ellen asked.

Charlie laughed. "He'll let us pull them out." He pulled Diamond a couple of yards to the left to study the bull.

Suddenly Charlie was aware that Ellen had dismounted. She was wearing Levis and a bright plaid riding shirt. The bull bellowed and shook his head. Trey Spot jumped back because Ellen had not dropped the reins to ground-hitch her. Charlie was startled. What was Ellen thinking of, dismounting in the face of an angry bull? Ellen realized that she had made a mistake, but instead of running to Charlie, she started back down the trail after Trey Spot, thinking she could catch the mare and mount.

The bull shook his head, and then he charged straight after Ellen. Charlie came to life in a flash. He set his spurs, shaking out his rope as the horse whirled about. Diamond knew what to do—he plunged forward as Charlie swung his rope. There wasn't time for a nice balancing of the loop, but Charlie flexed his wrist, and the loop dropped over the head of the bull. Charlie spoke to Diamond as he took a hitch around the saddle horn. Diamond slowed, then sat down, snapping the rope taut. The bull's head went down and his hindquarters came up. He was flipped neatly and landed with a thud on his side.

Charlie was out of the saddle instantly. He went down the rope and landed on the head of the bull. The bull kicked, but he could not get to his feet. Ellen stood, white-faced and shaken, looking at Charlie. He grinned at her.

"Lesson number one," he said. "Never go near an angry range bull on foot."

"Why did Trey Spot run away?" Ellen asked.

"You must always drop the reins to the ground. If you leave them around the horn, the horse will think you want her to go home. That's probably what Trey Spot has done," Charlie said.

"What are you going to do with the bull?" Ellen asked.

"I can't pull the quills out without help," Charlie said. "And I can't sit on his head much longer—he's getting really riled. You better climb the bank and hide in those bushes. I'll get back to Diamond."

"You won't get caught?" Ellen asked.

"No," Charlie said. "Diamond will see to that."

Ellen turned and ran up to the bushes. When she had vanished, Charlie slipped off the bull's head and ducked back to Diamond. He mounted, and when the bull scrambled to his feet, Charlie shook the noose loose. He would have to get Tex to help him rope and throw the bull so the quills could be pulled out. The animal was valuable. Grandby had paid five hundred dollars for him when he was a calf.

The bull galloped away and Ellen came out of the bushes.

"I have a lot to learn," she said. "Walking back to the ranch will teach me a lesson."

"You don't have to walk. Diamond will ride us double. We'll try to catch up with Trey Spot. If she gets to the ranch without a rider, the folks will worry." Charlie reached down to give Ellen a hand up.

BIG RED'S HAREM

CHARLIE had to help with the calf branding. Every day he fretted and watched the sky for a light plane. He saw no plane, but he knew it would come. The day the branding was over, Judge Hansen's daughter drove out to the ranch. She took Ellen into town for a week's visit.

As soon as Ellen left, Charlie headed for the high country. The sun was only an hour high when he reached the first benches below Horse Thief Pass. Charlie knew a lot about wild horses. He knew that the mares did not stay with Big Red because they loved him; they stayed because he could protect them, and because they were afraid of his slashing teeth and heavy hoofs. He was a tough master, punishing deserters savagely, but always ready to turn just as savagely upon an enemy, and he had the cunning of an old veteran of the range. Hackett had his work cut out for him, all right.

Charlie decided that Big Red knew everything about light planes that a wild horse needed to know. And he felt sure Big Red had returned to Bar L range after charging up the pass.

There was another angle that interested Charlie. The palomino colt was fast growing into a mature stallion who would challenge Big Red if he wasn't driven off. He was sure a deadly battle would be fought any time the colt decided to make a stand.

Charlie got his first break within an hour after reaching the horse range. He discovered the golden colt cropping grass at the edge of a meadow. Big Red could keep the mares under cover, but he could do nothing about the colt, who had not learned wariness.

Charlie worked his way to the windward of the colt. He was careful because there was no way of knowing when he might ride up on the mares feeding under cover. As he rode up on him, the thought came to Charlie that the golden colt probably stayed in the open so that Big Red couldn't trap him.

He was about to move on in search of the herd when the sound of an airplane engine broke the stillness. The plane seemed to be flying low and it was swinging around the slope. Charlie expected to see the colt break for cover, but the palomino kept on feeding. He was sure it was Hackett's plane and he didn't want Hackett to see the colt.

Charlie galloped Trey Spot toward the colt. He jerked his carbine from its boot and fired over the head of the colt. The palomino broke and ran, not into the timber but straight across the open meadow. The plane swooped down over him and up. Then it banked and came back low over Charlie. Hackett leaned out and shook a fist at Charlie.

Charlie heard Big Red's scream. It came from the same stand of timber Charlie was in. He caught a glimpse of the big fellow, standing at the edge of the timber. Big Red seemed to know the colt had betrayed him, and he was in a rage.

Charlie sat and waited. He had a feeling Hackett wasn't going to get the herd unless they were stampeded over the pass and into open desert country. The drone of the plane died away. He decided that he would not disturb the herd or the colt. He'd talk his father into letting him have Tex and Shorty for a day. They'd catch the colt and take him to the ranch.

As Charlie rode in to the ranch barn, he saw a light plane in the level meadow below the barn. Hackett had his nerve, making a landing on the Bar L! He'd make sure his father didn't let the horse hunter use the pasture as a base from which to hunt.

Two men were standing near the corral, talking to his father and Shorty. One of them was Hackett. When he pulled up at the corral gate, the two men turned and stared at him. Charlie swung down and dropped Trey Spot's reins. Grandby Carter spoke and his voice was curt.

"This man says you shot at his plane with your saddle gun."

Charlie stared back at his father. Then he said in a voice as cold as his

father's, "That's a lie! A downright lie! I did not shoot at his plane."

"There's a bullet hole in it," his father stated grimly.

Charlie stared at Hackett. Hackett was glowering at him. "You not only shot at us, you hit the plane. That's a criminal offense."

"I fired over the colt's head to scare him into the timber," Charlie answered. "Your plane wasn't even near the colt."

"There, that puts a lie to your yarn," Shorty said. His lips were thrust out and his hands were on his hips.

"You keep out of this," Grandby said.

"No use lying about it. Buck will swear the kid shot at us, and we can show the bullet hole," Hackett said.

"I didn't put a bullet through your plane," Charlie said. He turned and picked up Trey Spot's reins. Before he led the mare away, he turned to his father. "If there's a bullet hole in that plane, Hackett put it there himself to frame me."

Grandby Carter did not reply. He disliked Hackett, and just now the hunter had a smile on his fat lips. He turned and walked away.

A few minutes later the plane took off. It zoomed low over the horse corral, its motor roaring, the prop wash blasting dust around the horses. The horses stampeded wildly toward the near fence. Grandby ran out of the barn, while Shorty shook his fist at the departing plane. Grandby stopped beside Charlie at the corral gate.

"I guess he doesn't want you upsetting his plans," he said.

"I'll upset them," Charlie answered grimly.

THE CONTEST

CHARLIE spent some time riding the high country and studying the golden colt. He decided he would call the stallion Golden Boy. He watched and waited, wanting to study the habits of the herd and of the colt. It was clear that Golden Boy was beginning to mature. Twice he tried to steal mares from the herd and would have succeeded if the mares had been able to run as fast as he could. Then one day Charlie decided it was time to try out a plan he had decided upon.

He started out riding Diamond and trailing Trey Spot and a pack horse. He was off before dawn and reached the high benches by the time the sun rose. He did not want Big Red to know he was in the barrens. With a string of three horses, he had to move carefully.

When he had located the herd, he left Diamond concealed in a stand of aspen trees. He led Trey Spot into the open and picketed her in a small clearing, removing her halter and using only a nose loop to hold her. Returning to Diamond, he mounted. From the grove to where Trey Spot was feeding was only a short distance. If Golden Boy saw the mare, he would come to her and either try to make friends or drive her away. Charlie would be close enough to drop a rope on him.

Charlie knew that Big Red held the mares on a bench near a canyon while Golden Boy stayed higher up where he was safe. Finally Charlie spotted the herd. They were moving slowly up from the lower end of the bench. He could see Big Red, but he caught no glimpse of Golden Boy. He began to worry. If the herd got closer, he'd have to move Trey Spot or risk a brush with Big Red. Finally Big Red turned the mares and headed them down into a ravine.

The herd disappeared with Big Red pausing for a last look across the bench. The mares were barely out of sight when Golden Boy appeared at a swift gallop. Big Red moved below the hill, but the colt did not follow the herd into the ravine, which indicated that Big Red might be just out of sight and too close for the colt to attempt going into the ravine.

Then Golden Boy saw Trey Spot. He broke into a fast trot and swept into the clearing, nickering eagerly. Charlie shook out his rope and Diamond tensed himself for a charge. Golden Boy swerved just before he reached the mare. He slid to a halt and extended his muzzle toward her. She laid back her ears warningly.

Suddenly Charlie half-turned in his saddle. Big Red had come back out of the ravine. The leader paused to stare at the two horses in the clearing. Then with a savage challenge he charged up the slope. Charlie sat tight. He did not want to send Big Red and the herd thundering away with Golden Boy following.

Golden Boy had a decision to make. He could stay and fight or he could try to drive the mare away ahead of him, hoping they could outrun Big Red. He decided to try to get her away.

Whirling, he leaped at the mare and sunk his teeth into her rump. With a squeal of pain Trey Spot leaped away from those teeth. She hit the end of the picket rope and that slowed her a little. Then the nose loop slipped, and the rope shot away from her. She started running with Golden Boy racing at her side.

Big Red thundered after the pair. He was fast, a lot faster than Charlie

would have believed. He could not overtake Golden Boy, but he was gaining on Trey Spot. The palomino saw what was happening. He whirled and dodged into the path of the charging leader.

They crashed together at the rim of the mesa and this time the youngster did not go down. It was Big Red who stumbled and plunged to the left. Instantly Golden Boy lunged again. Big Red fought to keep his balance, but he was sent slipping and stumbling down into the ravine.

Charlie eased Diamond into the clear. He thought he saw a chance to rope the colt, now that the battle was over. Diamond charged down upon the colt as he stood staring down into the ravine.

As Diamond charged in, Charlie swung his loop and it landed neatly around the colt's neck. Diamond slid to a halt and put his weight on the rope, tightening the noose, keeping the pressure on to shut off the colt's wind.

But Golden Boy did not act the way a wild bronco should when roped. As soon as the rope bit into his neck, instead of tugging and trying to pull away, he lunged straight at Diamond. The instant he leaped, there was slack on the rope and the noose loosened.

There was nothing Charlie could do except save Diamond from a bad smashing. He loosed the hitch around the saddle horn and tossed the rope aside, leaning far to the side to help Diamond escape the charge of the wild-eyed palomino. But fast as he was, Diamond could not get away clean. Golden Boy hit him as he pivoted, and he went down.

Charlie was thrown clear. He rolled over and scrambled to his feet. He stood watching the colt. Within four strides, he had shaken loose the rope and was running beautifully, straight toward Trey Spot, who had halted and was watching him. As he drew near, she turned and fled, remembering his sharp teeth. He overtook her and shouldered her toward the timber. Charlie picked up his hat and slapped the dust from it. Then he started to laugh. Golden Boy had not only beaten him, he had stolen his saddle mare.

Charlie recovered his rope and mounted Diamond. He took up the trail of the pair. He felt pretty good. Trey Spot would help him capture the stallion. Hours later his good humor had vanished. He could follow their trail, but he could not overtake the pair. What he did not like was the direction Golden Boy was taking. He should have been swinging in a great circle which would keep him in the barrens. What he was doing was heading south toward the desert in an almost straight line.

Charlie was faced with a decision. He could keep on and sleep out supperless and without blankets, or he could go back and pick up his pack horse. He decided that returning to the pack horse was the sensible thing to do.

While Charlie slept, Golden Boy pushed on. Trey Spot soon discovered that she could not escape from the golden stallion. He now had the beginning of a herd, and he had no intention of letting her escape. If he returned to the breaks, Big Red might capture her and add her to his harem. The only other place he knew lay to the south, so he kept Trey Spot moving down through the foothills toward the desert. He kept pushing on into the dry wasteland even after the sun rose and heat waves danced on the horizon.

Wind swirled sand over the barren ground and covered the tracks the pair made. Trey Spot was desperately hungry and thirsty, but Golden Boy did not halt until they reached a deep canyon where the sandstorm was only a whisper. There were scattered bunches of tough grass and a bitter spring under a ledge. Here they stopped.

This was a place Big Red had discovered, a hideout from Navajo horse hunters. No Navajo would enter the canyon because of the deserted houses of the cliff dwellers. They called it the Canyon of the Dead.

When Charlie reached the edge of the desert the next day, he knew it was useless to go on. A vast land spread below him. The sandstorm had swept away all tracks. Sadly he turned back and headed for home.

Grandby Carter was not well-pleased when Charlie reported what had happened. He figured he now had two wild stallions to contend with. He wished he had not ordered Hackett off his land. But Charlie was hopeful. The golden stallion would return and he would capture him.

DESERT CHASE

TREY SPOT and Golden Boy soon discovered that the bunch grass in the Canyon of the Dead was getting scarce. After the lush meadows of the high country, it afforded only a starvation diet. Within a few weeks Golden Boy was ready to make a change. Hunger and a desire to build up a herd of his own made him leave the canyon.

The country Golden Boy and Trey Spot set out to explore was Navajo country. Among the Navajos, the sheep and goats, the hogan and the children, all belong to the women. The horses belong to the men. No Navajo man is considered important unless he has horses.

Golden Boy made his first raid on a herd belonging to Willie Yellow Man. He stole five mares and drove them into the hills a few miles from Willie's hogan.

Willie Yellow Man discovered the theft at once, and by reading signs knew exactly what had happened. He called in the men of his clan and they planned a horse hunt. The capture of even two horses interested the Navajos.

The Navajo riders scattered in every direction over the desert. Willie and his uncle, Tom Begay, and Willie's son, Bekis, took the trail of the stallion. Golden Boy and his mares were not difficult to find. The mares were not wild horses, and lacked the wariness of horses born wild. Willie located the herd just before sunset the first day out.

"The big stallion I want," Tom Begay said.

Willie just grunted. Bekis said, "The mare has a brand." He liked the looks of Trey Spot very much. "I want the mare."

The hunters built a small fire and sent a smoke signal into the sky to let the other hunters know the herd had been found and where it was.

Very soon dusky riders began closing in on the wash where Golden Boy held his herd. There were sixteen men and eleven boys in the band. Some had saddles and bridles, others rode bareback and guided their horses with rope hackamores. The mounts were bony, but they were tough.

The Navajos had a simple plan for catching wild horses. The idea was to run them in relays of fresh riders, to keep them from water, food or sleep until they were fagged out and could be easily caught.

Golden Boy sensed that something was wrong. He stood on a dune watching the mares as they moved restlessly about seeking a few bunches of grass. Suddenly the silence was broken by wild shouts. Where there had been nothing but rocks and scrub sage, there appeared a band of Navajos.

Golden Boy leaped toward his herd. He lashed at the mares in an attempt to stampede them. Startled more by his screaming attack than by the approaching riders, they raced away. Golden Boy kept them bunched and running fast for more than a mile. Golden Boy and Trey Spot could easily leave the Navajos behind, but the Indian mares did not put any heart into the flight. He lashed at them and shouldered them. They refused to stay bunched and soon two of them dropped out. Within another mile the stallion had to let the other three drop out. With Trey Spot racing at his side, the Indians were soon left far behind.

As the Navajos had expected, Golden Boy ran in a great circle. He kept running until long after the last Navajo had faded from sight. At last he halted on a high ridge to let Trey Spot blow. Before she had taken a second breath, five riders appeared out of a wash nearby.

Golden Boy and Trey Spot were off again. Again the riders were quickly left behind. He stayed on his circle course so as to keep within familiar range. The second time he halted to let the mare catch her breath, they were charged by three riders. The shrill cries of the three hunters let the other Navajos know where the horses were. Golden Boy and Trey Spot fled again.

Now they needed water, so Golden Boy headed for a spot where he knew they could get a drink. They plunged down a bank toward a pool which gleamed muddy yellow in the moonlight. Suddenly four tall forms rose from the ground close to the water hole. The shouting started again. The guards at the water hole did not follow, but two riders took up the chase just over the rim.

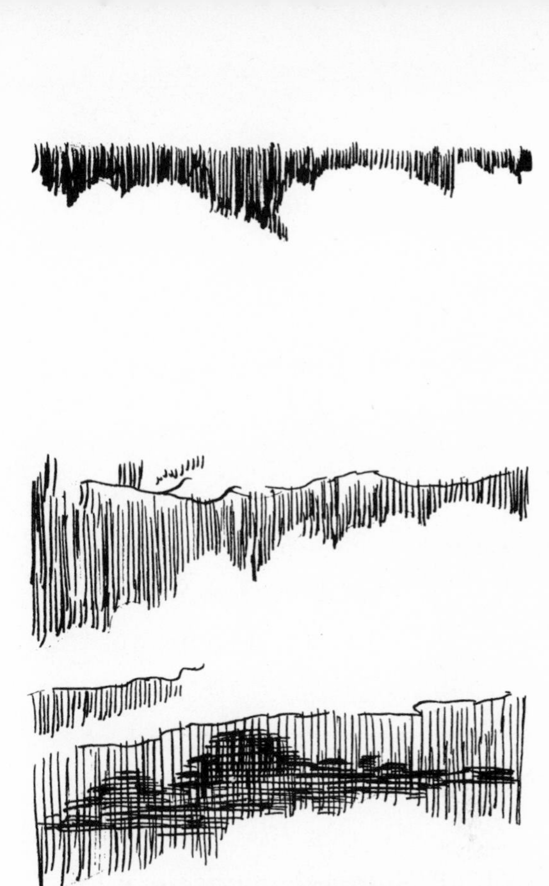

They got nothing to drink. The Navajos knew every watering place. At the second water hole there were only two boys, but they yelled as loudly as the men. Fifty yards from the water hole three riders tried to cut Trey Spot away from Golden Boy, but he drove her between them and on across an open mesa.

Trey Spot was past caring when he nipped her flanks. She plodded on because she wanted to escape from the yelling Navajos and because she had the heart to put up a fight. But she was near exhaustion.

It was Willie and Tom Begay who had taken up the chase the last time. They kept on the trail of the pair because they knew the mare was weakening. They did not hurry, but they did not lose the trail.

By the time daylight came, Trey Spot was stumbling. Golden Boy halted on a knoll. He was expecting riders to appear, and they came out of an arroya to the south. While Tom had kept on trailing the pair, Willie had joined Bekis and cut across the circle to wait at a likely spot.

Willie shook out his rope eagerly. Bekis bent forward to uncoil his own rope. They would try for the mare. If she was tired enough, they might overtake her.

Golden Boy broke and, as he leaped, he tried to push Trey Spot into a gallop. She made a noble attempt and for a hundred yards she pulled away from Willie and Bekis. But they were mounted on their best horses and those horses were fresh.

They bore down on Trey Spot, swinging their ropes. Both loops settled over her head. The instant she felt the ropes, she stopped running. She was too well trained to fight a rope. Bekis was the first to reach her. He rode close to her side and laid a hand on her shoulder. Trey Spot shook her head wearily. She was glad to feel the touch of a friendly hand.

Golden Boy easily ran away from Willie and Tom. He sent a wild call ringing back to the mare, but she did not answer. He now abandoned the circle course and headed north toward the distant mountains. He kept going as the sun mounted higher and higher and the desert heat became intense.

Toward evening Golden Boy came to a narrow valley which was heavily timbered. He knew he could go no farther without water. He blew dust from his nostrils and took a deep breath. Slowly he moved toward a big cottonwood tree in the bottom. He could smell willow and willow meant water. Weary as he was, he moved warily, keeping himself ready for a fast break if the water was guarded. Nothing happened.

Inside a grove he found a pool of clear water. He plunged in and thrust his muzzle deep into the cool water. But he did not drink heavily at first.

Golden Boy stayed near the pool a few days, feeding and drinking. On the third day he looked up at the mountains. They seemed very close. A strong desire to return to the high country seized him. He missed Trey Spot, and he needed to find mares he could lead. The short, high country summer was slipping away. He felt he must hurry. So he loped up a slope toward the mountains.

THE CHALLENGE

GOLDEN BOY moved up through the cow range into the broken ridges of the spruce belt. He was sleek and full of energy. Entering the breaks, he worked his way from park to park, and then began checking the little mesas higher up. He did not find Big Red in any of the places where the herd had stayed while he was with them. Big Red had led the mares into higher, more inaccessible country.

At last he located the herd in a snug valley. Big Red had picked the valley as a refuge, not against man, but against the coming winter. It was a box canyon circled by high rims. At the upper end, a stream flowed through a narrow slash in the walls. At the lower end, the walls closed to the very edge of the stream, forming a gateway. Here the herd could be held easily when the storms came.

Golden Boy splashed through the gateway where the stream flattened into a wide riffle. He would not have entered but for the horse smell which funneled down out of the canyon. He sent a shrill challenge ringing upward. It echoed along the cliff walls and the mares heard it. Big Red heard it, and his angry answer came echoing back to the young palomino as he arched his neck and galloped upward. He plunged through a stand of scrub oak and swept around a small beaver lake to break into the open at the edge of a long meadow.

Swinging to his right, he came to a halt on a grassy knoll. Big Red stood at the edge of a balsam grove where he had been sunning himself. For a moment he stood staring across at the golden stallion. For once Big Red hesitated before breaking to the attack. No longer was this youngster a colt who could be driven off. He must be smashed and broken.

As they faced each other, the sun which had been shining a few minutes before was dimmed and a cold shadow swept across the narrow meadow. Low scudding clouds fanned out from the rims above. Then the wind they were riding sucked down into the valley. The blast was icy cold. For a moment it caused the two stallions to pause because it was the breath of a common enemy.

Golden Boy was the first to move. Shaking his head, he sounded his challenge. Big Red answered and they both leaped forward. As their bodies crashed together, the first wall of driven snow swirled around them. The mares turned their backs to the blast and to the battle, lowering their heads

as they humped their backs. Big Red and Golden Boy did not notice the snow at all. They had rocked backward after the first impact. Big Red's teeth ripped at the youngster's neck, and blood darkened the blond chest. Golden Boy smashed him with heavy hoofs. Big Red grunted savagely as the blows battered him. He reared and struck back.

Then, as though at a signal from an unseen referee, they whirled and separated. Without pause they charged again, and their bodies met in solid jarring impact, solid flesh and bone against solid flesh and bone. Their hoofs lashed out and their teeth snapped savagely. Their maddened cries rose above the wail of the storm. Golden Boy was faster and landed more blows, but Big Red was heavier and he was driven by the fury of desperation. He seemed to sense that this was his last great battle.

Again and again they crashed together, screaming and slashing. Golden Boy felt the blows, but not the pain. He was filled with a fury which would not be denied. Big Red felt the impact and the pain very little, but he did feel the weakness in his legs which was slowing his attack. Slowly he began to give ground. As he backed away, Golden Boy drove in even more savagely, battering him back step by step.

With a last desperate rally, Big Red hurled himself at Golden Boy, catching the youngster off balance. Flushed with success, he sent the young stallion staggering backward. Then, following up the advantage, he was on Golden Boy with all the fury left in him. Golden Boy gave ground until he could get set. Then he charged.

Big Red stumbled back as Golden Boy leaped at him with an attack as powerful as his first rush had been. A great weariness was creeping through the scarred veteran's body. He was barely able to defend himself and could give no thought to attack. Slowly he retreated down the valley. Golden Boy was fresh and eager to finish his rival, but Big Red stubbornly refused to go down. He kept moving back, weaving and staggering, but staying on his feet.

He retreated around the beaver lake and into the shallows of the stream. Suddenly Golden Boy stopped as though he expected Big Red to charge him, but Big Red backed through the gateway and into the wall of swirling snow.

Big Red limped along through the storm. He was staggering, not caring where he was headed. Like many a stallion that he had battered and smashed in the days of his prime, he was retreating to some lonely spot where he could recover from his wounds.

An old she-wolf and her three dogs caught the smell of blood as he limped past a ledge where they were howling into the storm. They were hungry and the smell of blood meant that a cripple was near. They raced through the swirling snow, fanned out and closed in upon the stallion. Big Red did not see them until they were upon him. He backed slowly around to face them. But he could not face all of them and he was weak. Within minutes it was over and the wolves were feeding.

Up in the valley, Golden Boy was prancing about, showing off for the benefit of the mares. They admitted his leadership, but showed no signs of response to his playfulness. They were more concerned about the long winter they faced.

WHITE FAMINE

WHITE death faced many of the dwellers of the high country after the snows came. The old wolf and her sons were always hungry. They ran far, but their kills were few. The cougars made long foraging trips deeper and deeper into the lower country. Only the bears enjoyed the winter. Years ago they had given up the battle against the white famine. They curled up in a cave and lived off the fat stored under their hides during the summer.

Golden Boy and the mares dug down through the snow to uncover dry grass and small shrubs. They foraged on willow and alder twigs growing along the frozen stream. Their ribs pushed against their shaggy hides, raising ridges. Their new leader stood by, ready to drive away wolves or cougars.

Two of the older mares lay down during a storm and never got to their feet again. They went to sleep and the bitter cold crept through their bodies, lulling them into a numbness from which they could not be roused by the stallion. For a time after that storm, the wolf and her sons feasted upon frozen horse meat.

One day, one of the colts wandered from the herd to an overhanging ledge. On the ledge a cougar had been keeping watch for many hours, hoping that a colt would wander near. When the colt paused to nip at a bush clinging to the rock, the cougar leaped. One blow killed the colt. Golden Boy came plunging through the snow to the rescue. The cougar leaped back and climbed a tree. In the end the cougar got its meal, but Golden Boy kept it up the tree for a long time.

His fury that day was a beautiful thing to see. He smashed at the trunk of the tree. He tore great holes in the snow. The cougar lay on a limb, its yellow eyes following the stallion, no part of it moving except the black tip of its tail.

Even the snowy owls suffered from the famine. The grouse burrowed down under the snow, and even the rabbits refused to venture out of the willow thickets. The owls beat along the edge of the timber at dusk, their round glassy eyes watching for any sign of movement. In their savage hunger, they attacked any living thing.

Down on the desert, to the south, the winter was not too severe, but forage for horses was not plentiful. Bekis did the best he could for Trey Spot. He was very proud of the mare and treated her very well, according to Navajo standards. He easily won every race they entered. He was considered a very wealthy boy because he owned such a fine horse.

Trey Spot did not take readily to Navajo ways. She missed her grain and the rack of timothy hay. But she was better off than she had been in the desert with Golden Boy. Bekis spent much time with her and tried to see that she found the best grass. He dared not turn her loose with Willie Yellow Man's horses because he was afraid she would head for home.

When he knew she was going to have a foal, he was very much excited. The colt would belong to him. Everyone knew it would be a fine colt because its father was the great golden stallion.

Back at the Bar L, Charlie would not have worried so much about Trey Spot if he had known that she was in the hands of a Navajo boy. He was sure she must be snow-locked in some valley where the drifts were piled high. He was afraid such a high-spirited mare could not survive a range winter. Trey Spot had never had to forage for herself. He did not talk about her, but he often thought of her, and once he wrote about her to Ellen.

SPRING

Spring came slowly to the high country. In the sheltered valley where Golden Boy held his mares, the snow melted from the open meadows before it vanished from the less sheltered parts of the range. With new grass and weeds shoving up tantalizing stems, the mares became restless. They could smell the new grass, but could only get a taste. They would have wandered far, seeking better pastures, if Golden Boy had let them.

Some instinct kept the golden stallion in the valley. March storms, with a brief return of winter, proved him wise. He liked the security of the towering cliffs which walled his retreat. It reminded him of the canyon of death far to the south.

Spring brought a revival of life in the wild country. The coyotes ran in pairs and the big cats prowled and fought noisy love fights under the stars. The little folk of the bush came out and frisked about. The stark shadow of hunger faded with the coming of warm days. A shaggy old bear came down out of a cave on the south wall. He looked gaunt and hungry, but all he ate when he first appeared was a few mouthfuls of dirty snow. Golden Boy watched him warily, but he did not attack him.

When the grass was tall enough for grazing, Golden Boy let the herd leave the valley and feed on the meadows below. But he held them near enough to the refuge so that he could stampede them into it if need be.

It was while they were grazing in a park below the valley that Charlie and Shorty sighted them. They were not looking for wild horses, and they rode out of the timber and came upon the herd unexpectedly. They sat and watched Golden Boy stampede the mares up a small stream and into heavy timber. Shorty looked at Charlie.

"You were right. That young stallion is some horse," he said.

"I'll say he's some horse, but he's no wild one," Charlie said. Then he added sadly, "Trey Spot wasn't with them."

"No." Shorty frowned. "Probably didn't make it through the winter. Notice how poor those mares are?"

"Yeah," Charlie agreed. He felt sad about Trey Spot, but excitement filled him. The golden stallion was back. He'd return and watch the herd. Perhaps he could figure out a way to capture Golden Boy.

Shorty knew what Charlie was thinking. He smiled, but he did not say anything. He had an itch to catch the stallion himself.

The morning Charlie set out to locate the wild herd again, he was up before daybreak. He cinched an outfit on a pack horse. He used the excuse that he was going after the old wolf and her sons. The boys had spotted the killers, and trouble was expected. He would watch for the wolves, but mostly he wanted to study the wild stallion.

He headed straight for the breaks and by mid-afternoon he was riding up Canna Creek, keeping a sharp watch for Golden Boy and his herd. He located them high up where Canna Creek flowed out of a tight valley. He got only a glimpse of the stallion because he wanted to get the wind just right and make sure he wasn't seen. He hitched the pack horse in heavy cover before moving around the herd.

His first good look at Golden Boy made his pulse pound. He was so taken with the stallion that he paid no attention to the mares. One of them moved into the aspen grove where Charlie was sitting. When she saw Diamond, she whinnied loudly and fled.

Golden Boy sounded the alarm and sent his herd upcountry. Charlie followed. He trailed the herd to the entrance to the tight valley. As he sat looking at the gateway, he remembered the box canyon. Golden Boy wasn't as wise as Big Red. He should have kept his herd in the open. Then he smiled broadly. If he could talk his father into making a drive, they could catch the stallion and his herd. He rode off without disturbing the herd.

That night at supper he announced, "I saw Golden Boy."

Grandby smiled. "You want to tempt me into a wild horse drive."

"I want to show you how easy it would be to take him. You'll want him as much as I do when you see him," Charlie said eagerly.

Grandby agreed to ride into the breaks and take a look at the stallion. They left early one morning and after Grandby had watched the palomino for ten minutes he turned to Charlie.

"He's worth catching," he said. And that settled the matter of a wild horse drive.

CANYON TRAP

ONCE the Bar L crew started out to trap the golden stallion, they devoted full time to the job. Two trail wagons started out for the box canyon. Charlie and Shorty rode ahead to scout the area and to wait for a chance to stampede the herd into the closed valley where they could be held until a trap was built at the narrow entrance. They hoped to have Golden Boy and his mares in the valley before the slow-moving wagons arrived at the entrance.

They located Golden Boy and his herd on Canna Creek. Charlie had worried all the way up the mountain for fear they wouldn't be there, but there they were, less than a mile below the box canyon. Now the question was, would Golden Boy seek escape into the canyon or break for the high country above it?

As they sat on a bushy knoll looking down into the valley, Shorty grinned. His eyes had not left the golden stallion. He had been breaking horses since he was sixteen, a full twenty-seven years. He considered himself retired, so far as wild horses went, but as he watched Golden Boy, he knew he wanted to gentle at least one more wild one before he was through.

"High-strung type," he said. "We'll gentle him without breaking his spirit. A hoss like that can't be beat into doing anything."

Charlie nodded. He had been dreaming of handling the stallion himself. He was aware it was just a dream. His father would insist that Shorty take charge.

"He'll take a saddle," he said.

Shorty nodded. "But, like they say about rabbit stew, you have to catch the rabbit first."

They separated and rode down to approach the herd from two different angles. Charlie had the shortest distance to go. He got set in a grove and waited for Shorty's signal.

When he heard the signal, he headed his horse, Blackie, out into the open. Shorty was galloping out of the woods on his right. Instantly, Golden Boy screamed and started bunching his mares. He sent them flying up the creek. Charlie and Shorty galloped after the herd, but did not make too much fuss.

"He ain't acting like Big Red," Shorty shouted.

"He isn't Big Red," Charlie agreed. "But he'll fight, I know."

Golden Boy pushed the herd through the gateway and on to the upper end of the canyon. He halted at the upper end of the beaver lake and watched the gateway. When no riders appeared, he joined the mares.

Charlie and Shorty took up positions at the entrance. The wagons arrived two hours later. Ann had ridden up with Grandby. She fixed lunch from a basket. Camp was set up below the entrance.

Up in the canyon Golden Boy heard the sound of axes. He galloped back and forth, his eyes on the slot below the beaver lake. After a bit, he galloped down to the beaver dam and saw Tex and Shorty setting heavy posts into the ground. With a wild scream, he whirled and raced back up the meadow. He would have stampeded the herd out of the canyon if there had been any other exit.

Down at the gateway, the men

had thrown up a fence across the opening. They lashed the last pole into place after dark by the light of a lantern. In the morning a second fence with a gate would be added to form a tight corral.

Golden Boy did not sleep. He rounded up his mares and headed them down the canyon, hoping to escape in the darkness. As he neared the gateway, he lashed them to a gallop. A bay mare was first to reach the pole fence. Snorting loudly, she whirled and charged back. Golden Boy slashed at her, but he soon found out why she had turned back. He let the mares retreat, but stood watching.

The next day the men finished the upper fence and gate. By nightfall the lower fence was hidden by branches so that the horses would not see it as they entered the gate.

An hour before dawn the next morning the Bar L boys set about putting their plan into action. Charlie rode his mother's horse, Diamond. Grandby stationed himself under cover near the beaver lake. If the herd outran the riders, he would charge out and make sure the stallion and his mares passed through the gate. Ann manned the trip rope which would close the gate.

The riders reached the upper end of the valley and spread out to circle the herd. Charlie rode beside Tex. As light came, they spotted the herd. The cowboys shouted and fanned their hats. Golden Boy was startled at seeing riders coming from above. He rushed at the mares, crying loudly. They stampeded down the meadow.

Golden Boy made a real show out of the stampede. He leaped from mare to mare, snapping savagely at their flanks and rumps. The herd thundered around the beaver lake and rushed into the gateway. Golden Boy was close behind them, urging them on. Charlie saw his father close in on the herd as Golden Boy pushed them through the gate.

The lead mares hit the lower fence and were hurled back. One mare went down and a colt was badly shaken. Golden Boy smashed against the fence, then whirled toward the gate which was still open. Charlie caught his breath. The gate trip must have stuck. He saw his mother standing up, pulling on the rope. She suddenly rushed down toward the gate, intent upon closing it by hand. It seemed she would surely be trampled by the charging stallion. Grandby Carter was the nearest rider to the gate. He set his spurs and charged toward it. He sent the horse against the stuck gate and it swung shut in Golden Boy's face. Ann sank to the ground as the big palomino hit the stout poles. Grandby dismounted and helped her to her feet.

EASY DOES IT

CHARLIE and Shorty made camp close to the corral. The branded mares had been cut out and would be returned to their owners. All of the wild mares except the bay were turned loose. Grandby had allowed Charlie and Shorty two weeks to gentle Golden Boy.

"When he starts eating grain and knows it comes from us, we'll have half of the battle won," Charlie said.

Shorty nodded. "Used to break six a day. He'll take the two weeks we have."

The first step was to get a rope on Golden Boy's forefeet. Shorty made the catch neatly. Golden Boy plunged and went down. Charlie leaped in and tied the forefeet securely. Shorty shook loose his rope, then he moved in and slipped a heavy halter over the stallion's head. There was a drag rope attached to the halter. Charlie jerked the loop and the hobble rope loose and leaped back.

Golden Boy plunged to his feet and dashed around the corral with the drag rope snaking behind him. The battle between the two men and the wild stallion was on. They sat in their saddles and watched Golden Boy fight the drag rope. When he finally halted, Shorty moved his horse toward him. He swung down and picked up the rope, then remounted and took a hitch around his saddle horn with the rope.

Golden Boy felt the rope jerk and leaped. Setting his weight against the rope, he dragged Shorty's horse forward. The horse planted his feet and held back stubbornly, but Golden Boy soon had him moving at top speed. They dashed toward a snubbing post planted in the center of the corral. Golden Boy charged past the post, but Shorty's horse did not pass on the same side. He went around the post like a scared rabbit, snubbing Golden Boy up close. Golden Boy fought the rope savagely, but he couldn't free himself.

Toward evening they loosened the drag rope from the post. Golden Boy had fought himself out. But he was still cagey and ready to fight. He dashed away with the rope jerking behind him. The contest went on, day after day. Charlie was able to get close to the stallion after a few days. He talked to him and finally got him to eat from a mound of oats.

The work went on and the day came when Golden Boy was hobbled and Charlie got his hands on him. The stallion screamed and fought, finally throwing himself. But after many tries, he calmed down and Charlie could put his hands on him without his fighting back.

Shorty made the first ride after Golden Boy had learned what a saddle was. The stallion bucked, but Shorty was an expert and stayed on top. Finally Golden Boy gave in. The next day Charlie rode him. By this time he had made friends with the big palomino. As soon as they started out, Charlie was sure he had a great horse who would obey his commands.

RODEO TIME

Rodeo time was drawing near. Charlie had high hopes that Golden Boy would win the big race. He had spent the last week before the rodeo running Golden Boy against the best horses the Bar L owned.

The rodeo at Cedar Bank was a typical cattleman's show. It was not a fair or an attraction to draw people from outside the cow region; it was a get-together where the ranchers met once a year.

Charlie had always entered the calf roping and the junior riding events. This year he would enter only the big race. In the championship race, any horse owned by a rancher or a cowboy could be entered.

The first day of the rodeo found Charlie in town with Golden Boy stabled near the grounds. There was a parade in the morning with bucking events and calf roping in the afternoon. A lot of visiting was done and some business deals were closed. Charlie rode Golden Boy in the parade. The stallion was nervous because of the crowds, but Charlie managed him. He wanted Golden Boy to get used to a crowd so that he would not be bothered at the race.

Shorty was riding beside Charlie, to be ready if there was any trouble with the stallion. Charlie got Golden Boy into place and took a look along the line of mounted men and women. His mother and father were up ahead. Diamond was dancing prettily, showing off himself and Ann. Suddenly he leaned toward Shorty.

"Look," he said, pointing to a horse four places ahead of them.

Shorty looked and saw a black mare with a buckskin filly at her side. An Indian boy was riding the mare bareback.

"An Indian—Navajo," Shorty said.

"It's Trey Spot," Charlie said, his voice almost a shout.

Shorty took a good look. "It shore is," he agreed.

"Golden Boy took her south into the desert. He came back without her. The Navajos must have caught her." Charlie was so excited he almost let Golden Boy get out of line.

The parade started to move and he had to give all of his attention to

Golden Boy. Trey Spot had been well cared-for. That made Charlie feel friendly toward the Navajo boy.

When the parade was over, Charlie saw the Navajo boy leave town and head for the Indian camp by the creek. He and Shorty followed. When they rode into the camp, Bekis was picketing Trey Spot on a grassy knoll. He looked at the brand on the two approaching horses and knew that one of them was the owner of the mare.

"Hello," Bekis said in English.

Charlie smiled down at the boy. "Fine mare you have there," he said.

"Yes," Bekis said.

"Do you think she'll win the race?" Charlie grinned at Bekis.

"She has always won," Bekis answered.

Golden Boy was fighting his bit and pricking his ears toward Trey Spot. Willie Yellow Man rode to where they were talking. He had been expecting trouble ever since they started taking the mare around to races.

Bekis spoke to Willie in Navajo. Willie nodded. He, too, had read the brands.

"This fellow," Charlie patted Golden Boy's neck, "stole my mare a year ago and returned from the desert without her." He looked at Trey Spot, then whistled.

It was a signal Trey Spot had obeyed since she was a filly. Her head came up and she whinnied eagerly as she pulled at her picket rope. Golden Boy started to prance. Charlie knew he'd better be going or he'd have trouble with the big fellow.

"Go ahead and race her. If she wins, the purse is yours," he said to Bekis. "I'll see you after the race, but we won't have any trouble over her."

For the first time, Bekis smiled. "She is a good horse," he said.

Charlie told his father about finding Trey Spot. Grandby suggested that Charlie take the mare but leave the colt for Bekis. The colt would certainly develop into a fine horse. That was the way matters stood when Charlie rode out to enter the big race.

At a mile, only good horses could be expected to bid for top honors. A horse had to have bottom, as the cowboys put it, to go the distance. There were a number of entries whose owners weren't talking much about their horses, but who had high hopes. Among the Lazy Y entries were two which they were backing heavily. The Circle M had one they were putting their money on. It wasn't a Bar L race by any means.

The track was a half-mile oval, which meant that the horses had to go two laps to complete the race. The track was dusty and plowed up in places by bucking horses and wild steers. As Charlie rode past the stands, he saw his mother. She waved at him.

There was considerable commotion at the starting line, where the judges and the official starter and a couple of cowhands were trying to finish the drawing for places. Golden Boy had drawn third place from the rail. Charlie held the stallion back and waited.

Bekis arrived with Trey Spot and drew the rail position. Charlie grinned at the young Navajo and Bekis smiled back.

"Get them straightened out," the starter shouted.

The horses were straightened out. None were hard to handle because they were all well trained range horses. Charlie held Golden Boy back. The starter waved him up to the line.

"I'll start from here," Charlie called.

"Take the handicap if you want to." The starter was rather relieved because he wasn't sure the big stallion would behave if he was crowded close to the other horses. Stallions dislike other male horses.

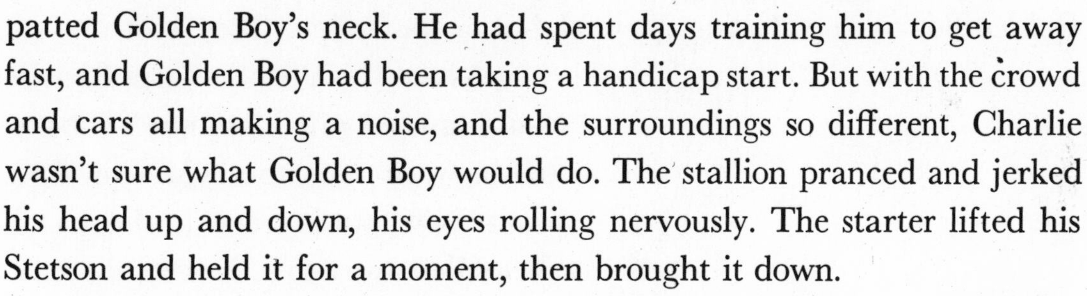

Charlie leaned forward and patted Golden Boy's neck. He had spent days training him to get away fast, and Golden Boy had been taking a handicap start. But with the crowd and cars all making a noise, and the surroundings so different, Charlie wasn't sure what Golden Boy would do. The stallion pranced and jerked his head up and down, his eyes rolling nervously. The starter lifted his Stetson and held it for a moment, then brought it down.

The horses broke and raced away, their riders whooping and swinging their quirts. Golden Boy watched them go for a full five seconds before he broke and raced after them. He gave voice to a shrill cry as he leaped forward. With a herd of horses out in front of him, he felt a wild urge to run.

He closed the gap quickly. The horses ahead were bunched at the first turn. Trey Spot was flying along with Bekis lying low on her neck and talking to her, but not using his quirt. As they whirled into the turn, Charlie began looking for an opening to shove Golden Boy through. The opening came on the far turn, but Golden Boy did not move up. He was satisfied in bringing up the rear, where a good herd leader belonged.

Charlie urged him and coaxed him, but Golden Boy just raced along behind the bunched horses. He even made a pass at a piebald who had dropped back. The piebald moved up at once. Charlie tried the quirt, but Golden Boy paid no attention to it.

As they swept into the stretch in front of the grandstand, Charlie began to see why the Lazy Y had extra horses in the race. Trey Spot was boxed in while one of the Lazy Y geldings was moving out in front, pushed closely by a Circle M entry, a lanky roan. Charlie watched Trey Spot anxiously. She would need four lengths lead when she reached the final stretch, where she would begin to weaken, but she wouldn't get it if they kept her penned in on the rail.

Charlie pulled Golden Boy over into the dust, behind the Lazy Y rider who was holding a position beside Trey Spot. As the stallion swung in on the heels of the gelding, he screamed a warning and laid back his ears. Golden Boy did not like geldings. The rider glanced back and saw the stallion coming. He swung his horse wide, forgetting what he was supposed to be doing.

Bekis saw his chance and moved Trey Spot out and into the open, where she fled down the track, passing the Circle M roan and coming up alongside the Lazy Y horse. Charlie grinned. He might not be able to get Golden Boy to stop chasing the field, but he had helped Trey Spot.

As they hit the next turn, Charlie was disgusted with his mount's actions, but he wasn't downhearted. Trey Spot was moving out in front. In the stretch she pulled away to a five-lengths lead. The roan and the Lazy Y gelding were fighting it out for second place. Golden Boy galloped along effortlessly, eating a lot of dust but not minding it. He had plenty of breath to waste on wild whinnies.

As they went into the next turn, Charlie's heart sank. He wasn't going to be able to budge Golden Boy out of last place. The stallion wouldn't even let the fagged piebald drop back and quit. Charlie looked across at Trey

Spot flying along in the lead. He was glad she was out there, but he wanted Golden Boy up there with her, making a race out of it. Then an idea hit him. He raised his head and blasted a shrill whistle between his teeth. He might be able to get Trey Spot to coax Golden Boy through the bunched horses.

He whistled a second time and heard Trey Spot's answering whinny. Golden Boy heard it, too, and his head came up. He answered lustily, then started moving up. He slipped past the bunched horses easily and was soon running neck and neck with the roan and the Lazy Y gelding who were now pulling up on Trey Spot. He passed the pair and raced after Trey Spot. He had only a length to gain, because that was all the lead she had left. They swung into the last stretch with Golden Boy galloping along close to the mare's flank and making no effort to pull up beside her.

Charlie glanced back and saw the pair of geldings swing wide for the final sprint. They looked fresh and strong while Trey Spot was straining now and failing fast. They were coming up on the outside in a final rush, their riders using their quirts to get one last burst out of their mounts. Charlie knew they would pass Trey Spot before she could reach the finish line.

Golden Boy seemed to know Trey Spot was letting down. He reached over and nipped her sharply. She leaped forward and he nipped her again on the rump. Trey Spot responded as she had when he was driving her long ago during the horse hunt. She put on a burst of speed that pulled her away from the geldings. Golden Boy stayed close to her, nipping her flank when she slackened her pace. He sent her across the line two lengths ahead of the roan and the Lazy Y horse, while he himself came in second, a half-length behind the mare.

The crowd roared its approval. They were all horsemen and knew the ways of a wild stallion. Golden Boy had put on a show they would talk about for years. When Bekis pulled Trey Spot in and trotted her back to the judge's stand, Golden Boy was at her side prancing proudly, shaking his head and snorting as though he hadn't been in a gruelling race, but had been playing a pasture game. There was nothing Charlie could do to stop him. He shared her honors when she halted to receive the winner's ovation.

Shorty and Grandby came to Charlie's rescue and they got Golden Boy away from Trey Spot. Ann Carter rode up on Diamond. She pushed to Charlie's side, her eyes shining, but there was so much noise from the crowd that Charlie could not hear what she said. Shorty was grinning broadly, even though Golden Boy had cost him a month's wages.

Bekis came through the crowd on foot. Willie Yellow Man was caring for Trey Spot. He looked up at Charlie and smiled.

"I had to ride her neck to keep him from biting me," he explained. "It was the way he drove her on the desert when we caught her."

"I didn't do much of a job of handling him," Charlie said. "He did all of the handling himself."

"What will you do about the mare?" Bekis asked.

"She is my favorite horse outside of Golden Boy," Charlie said. "I want her, but you will keep the colt. He will be a fine fast horse."

"I have talked with my father," Bekis said. "I would like to have the colt. The mare is yours. My father says she never was mine."

"And you are to keep the prize money. I have told the judges to give it to you." Charlie held out his hand. Bekis stood close to Golden Boy as they shook hands. Then the young Navajo turned and walked away through the crowd to the judges' stand.

Before leaving the barn that night, Charlie stood near the door and looked at the two stalls nearest him. In one of them, Golden Boy stood munching hay, while in the other one, Trey Spot was nervously nibbling grain and keeping her eyes on the door. She missed her colt, who was out at the Navajo camp. The colt was now big enough to be on his own, but he was her first colt, and so she missed him. Charlie smiled.

"The home meadows will make you forget," he said.

He would be riding the sleek black mare again. Golden Boy would be a range stallion watching over the Bar L mares on the benches above the cattle range. It would be fine for the big palomino. Kelly would be retired and Golden Boy would be king at the Bar L.

Charlie closed the barn door and started up the street toward the hotel where the Carters were staying. He'd write Ellen a letter and tell her all about the big race, the one he had lost.